Butterfly's Bad Day

by Liza Charlesworth

ISBN: 978-1-338-89036-5

Designer: Cynthia Ng; Illustrated by John Lund

Copyright © 2023 by Liza Charlesworth. All rights reserved. Published by Scholastic Inc.

1 2 3 4 5 6 7 8 9 10   68   31 30 29 28 27 26 25 24 23 22

Printed in Jiaxing, China. First printing, January 2023.

■SCHOLASTIC

Butterfly was sweet and sunny yellow.
Most days, she felt VERY happy.
She fluttered through the garden
with a great big smile
and helped all her friends.

Uh-oh! Spider was grumpy because
he dropped his ice cream cone.
So what did Butterfly do?
She fluttered over and cheered
Spider up with a song.

3

"Thanks, pal!" said Spider.
"Your song made me feel SO much better."
"I am happy to help!" replied Butterfly
with a great big smile.

Uh-oh! Ladybug was grumpy because
her pink balloon floated away.
So what did Butterfly do?
She fluttered over and cheered
Ladybug up with a joke.

"Thanks, pal!" said Ladybug.
"Your joke made me feel SO much better."
"I am happy to help!" replied Butterfly
with a great big smile.

Butterfly loved helping her pals feel better.
But guess what?
Sometimes she felt grumpy, too.
Turn the page to learn why she's NOT smiling.

First, she spilled her bowl of honey.

Then, she bumped her head on a branch.

Then, she broke her favorite toy.

Then, she dropped her book in the mud.

Butterfly felt VERY grumpy
because she was having a bad day.
Did she want her friends to see
her sad and mad? NO WAY!
So, Butterfly crept into
a big purple flower to hide.

But guess what?
Spider and Ladybug were taking a walk
and spotted the big purple flower.
"Let's stop to smell it," said Spider.
"Great idea!" replied Ladybug.

Sniff, sniff…SURPRISE!
They saw Butterfly inside.
"Hi there, pal!" said Spider.
"What is new?" asked Ladybug.
Butterfly tried hard to smile….

But tears fell from her eyes.
"I'm SO sorry," cried Butterfly.
"I didn't want you to see me like this."
"It's OK to be unhappy," said Ladybug.
"Now we can cheer YOU up," said Spider.
Turn the page to learn what they did.

First, Spider wrote Butterfly a nice note.

Then, Ladybug gave her a honey lollipop.

Then, they all did a super silly bug dance.
They flipped and flopped.
They wiggled and giggled.
And guess what?

This time, Spider and Ladybug
were able to help Butterfly.
"Thanks, pals! You made ME feel
SOOOOOOOOOOO much better,"
she said with a great big smile.